PRAISE FOR M. L. BUCHMAN

Top 10 Romance of 2012, 2015, and 2016.

— BOOKLIST: THE NIGHT IS MINE, HOT POINT,
HEART STRIKE

One of our favorite authors.

— RT BOOK REVIEWS

Buchman has catapulted his way to the top tier of my favorite authors.

— FRESH FICTION

A favorite author of mine. I'll read anything that carries his name, no questions asked. Meet your new favorite author!

— THE SASSY BOOKSTER, FLASH OF FIRE

M.L. Buchman is guaranteed to get me lost in a good story.

— THE READING CAFE, WAY OF THE WARRIOR:
NSDQ

I love Buchman's writing. His vivid descriptions bring everything to life in an unforgettable way.

— PURE JONEL, HOT POINT

FIRST DAY EVERY DAY

A NIGHT STALKERS ROMANCE STORY

M. L. BUCHMAN

Buchman Bookworks

SIGN UP FOR M. L. BUCHMAN'S
NEWSLETTER TODAY

and receive:
Release News
Free Short Stories
a Free Book

Do it today. Do it now.
www.mlbuchman.com/newsletter

Other works by M. L. Buchman:

The Night Stalkers

MAIN FLIGHT
The Night Is Mine
I Own the Dawn
Wait Until Dark
Take Over at Midnight
Light Up the Night
Bring On the Dusk
By Break of Day

WHITE HOUSE HOLIDAY
Daniel's Christmas
Frank's Independence Day
Peter's Christmas
Zachary's Christmas
Roy's Independence Day
Damien's Christmas

AND THE NAVY
Christmas at Steel Beach
Christmas at Peleliu Cove

5E
Target of the Heart
Target Lock on Love
Target of Mine

Firehawks

MAIN FLIGHT
Pure Heat
Full Blaze
Hot Point
Flash of Fire
Wild Fire

SMOKEJUMPERS
Wildfire at Dawn
Wildfire at Larch Creek
Wildfire on the Skagit

Delta Force

Target Engaged
Heart Strike
Wild Justice

Where Dreams

Where Dreams are Born
Where Dreams Reside
Where Dreams Are of Christmas
Where Dreams Unfold
Where Dreams Are Written

Eagle Cove

Return to Eagle Cove
Recipe for Eagle Cove
Longing for Eagle Cove
Keepsake for Eagle Cove

Henderson's Ranch

Nathan's Big Sky

Love Abroad

Heart of the Cotswolds: England

Dead Chef Thrillers

Swap Out!
One Chef!
Two Chef!

Deities Anonymous

Cookbook from Hell: Reheated
Saviors 101

SF/F Titles

The Nara Reaction
Monk's Maze
the Me and Elsie Chronicles

Strategies for Success (NF)

Managing Your Inner Artist/Writer
Estate Planning for Authors

The events in this story occur 2 years after
Ghost of Willow's Past
(The Night Stalkers Story #1).

ix

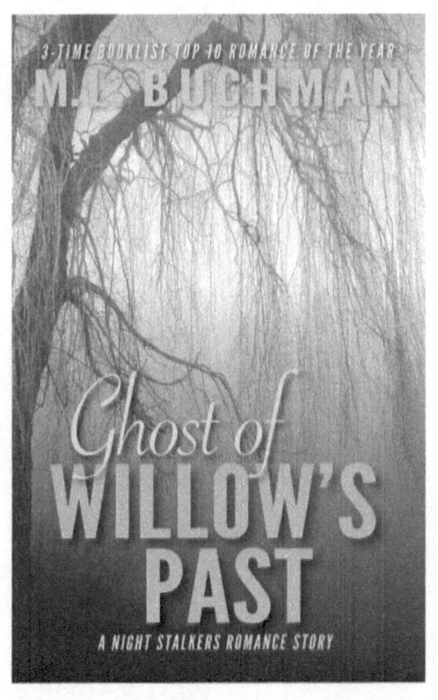

CHAPTER 1

Chief Warrant Officer Amelia Patterson-James felt the jarring impact before she spotted its origin. Standard 9mm rifle rounds would ping off her helicopter's windshield and armor with little effect. The only thing heavy enough to make the *Menace* jerk like this were anti-aircraft rounds, perhaps 23mm. Anything less wouldn't have jarred the helo; anything heavier and they wouldn't still be flying.

The *Menace* was an MH-6M Little Bird helicopter loaded for bear. Twin mini-guns and two seven-rocket tubes mounted outside on stub wings—the coolest office a girl could have. Inside there was room enough for only the pilot and co-pilot, and barely that. The cabin was so tight that the Little Birds were flown without doors, only the large front windshield offering any forward protection and not much of that.

Pilot? Amy felt the controls go loose in her hand. She'd been mirroring Bernie on her set of controls, and learning quite how good he was. It was her first sortie as co-pilot for the 5th Battalion D Company of the U.S. Army's 160th

SOAR, day one on the job after two years of training and five prior years of flying for lesser outfits.

Bernie, the pilot, wasn't reacting, which was a bad sign—no time to think about that.

Amy slammed the cyclic joystick that rose between her knees hard to the left and let *Menace* tumble into a sideways roll to get clear of the attack. It would make her harder to hit again; she just hoped that the helicopter was undamaged enough to recover from this roll or she was a dead woman. Her body alternately floated off the seat and slammed back onto it as the helo exchanged right side up for upside down and continued over.

Bernie flopped against her.

A very bad sign.

Pinning the cyclic between her thighs for a moment, she reached up and flicked the setting on his seatbelt harness that attached to the back of his vest. Now it was set to retract-only, like a car seatbelt, locking up during an emergency stop.

Grabbing the cyclic again in her right hand, she gave it a twist during the next tumble. Bernie flopped back against his seat, the harness retracted, and pinned him in place.

A quick glance revealed a hole punched through the left center of his visor. By the size of the hole, her estimate of the 23mm round was right on the money. The ultimate bad news for her pilot.

On your own, girl.

She didn't even have time to add a heartfelt, *Shit!* for Bernie's epitaph.

Amy returned her attention to the sharp granite mountains leading to the narrow mountain pass between Soran, Iraq and Piranshahr, Iran.

U.S. military forces weren't even supposed to be here.

This was a classic mission for the 160th Special Operations Aviation Regiment: Get in, hit the target, get the hell out.

Don't be seen.

Something the Night Stalkers of the 160th specialized in...usually.

The *don't be seen* part was easy. It was straight up midnight, two hours before moonrise. The anti-aircraft had caught them as much by chance as anything, firing wildly aloft after the two other helos ahead of her in the flight had roared by. They'd stirred up the hornet's nest and she and Bernie had walked right into it.

The three-bird flight had been flying down the gut of a river canyon. Now Amy was *falling* out of the sky *into* a river canyon and the rock walls were impossibly close through her night-vision goggles, glowing in a dozen shades of dull green in her infrared view.

She stomped on the left rudder and dragged the cyclic back to the right to break the roll.

The roll lashed back the other way and—once her eyes uncrossed from the g-force that drove her against her harness—she was able to focus on the fast-approaching rock of the steep canyon wall.

Menace groaned in protest, but responded.

Her baby wasn't supposed to groan.

Up on the collective with her left hand, craving a right turn through the sky with the cyclic in her right, she managed to skim along the wall with her skids barely a half-rotor diameter above the ground. Ripping along at a hundred-and-thirty knots—with rotor blades only twenty-seven feet in diameter—half a rotor was far too close for comfort.

That's when she spotted the attacker.

Her attacker.

The bastard nasty enough to think shooting her was a good idea.

Guess again, Jerkwad. You messed with the wrong girl.

Racing down the center of the narrow two-lane Iraq Route 3 that followed close beside the river was a white Toyota HiLux, the favorite vehicle of the world's rebels and terrorists. It was reliable as a rock and plenty powerful to carry the ton of weight of the twin-barrel, Russian ZU-23-2 anti-aircraft gun—that was even now trying to get a bead on her as the driver bounced and careened over the rough-paved road. There were two other gunmen in the back of the vehicle firing rifles in her direction. Bright sparks flashed before her as their bullets bounced off her windshield.

Without thought, courtesy of long training, Amy unleashed a pair of 70mm Hydra rockets up their tailpipe.

The first one creased the side of their truck and punched a hole in the hillside above the next curve in the road.

The second one delivered eight-point-seven pounds of high explosive as a direct hit on the tailgate. The rocket punched through the thin metal and delivered its full charge against the substantial anti-aircraft gun.

A fireball bloomed in a blinding green-white flash on her night vision gear, completely overloading the electronics and her optic nerves and obliterating all visibility.

Pull back on the cyclic.

Still dazzled by the explosion, she climbed to clear the aftermath and tried to recall if the thin power lines were on the north side of the road, or south.

North, she hoped, but wasn't sure. After the tumble she wasn't even sure whether she was flying east or west.

Toss the coin.

She pulled up and to the right. South.

Everything came apart at once.

Amy's vision came back in time to see and avoid the

telephone pole and line. It was also in time to witness one of her shot-up rotor blades break off at the midpoint. Instead of breaking away free, and giving the other five-and-a-half blades even a slim chance of survival, the titanium leading edge hung on long enough to slam the broken piece into her rear rotor.

With the rear rotor gone and her main rotor compromised, the helicopter whirled into an uncontrollable spin. On the third loop around, catching the power line with one of her skids was the least of her worries as her helmet slammed against a support strut. Knocked silly, Amy's head cleared while the helicopter was still swinging above the ground—upside down. She was dangling a dozen feet above the roadway, bobbing lightly up and down like some inverted carnival ride. The rotor blades, at least what remained of them, still spun below and were now blocking her escape. There'd be no jumping to get clear.

CHAPTER 2

There was an ominous crack.

The power pole she was caught on snapped from dry rot, not to mention having a ton and a half of helicopter slam into it.

The helo dropped, upside down, onto the boulder field close beside the narrow two-lane roadway. That took care of the lethal rotor at least. *Menace's* last act was to roll slowly onto its side so that her exit was now blocked by the road's surface.

With the death of her console, the information normally projected on the inside of her visor blinked out and took the night-vision gear with it. Amy raised her visor and switched to battery-powered night-vision goggles.

She lay with one shoulder on the ground, still strapped into her seat. Above her, Bernie dangled in his harness. A finger against his throat confirmed what she already knew.

She slapped her chest to assure herself that her rifle and survival vest were still there. Then she punched a fist against the harness release and was free.

Through the cracked glass-laminate of the wide windshield all she could see was boulders and a stretch of road. The canyon was well lit by the blazing truck somewhere out of view behind her. She stood up, impressed that her legs were still working and stuck her head out of Bernie's door to scan around. She felt like a meerkat popping up out of its burrow to scan for danger.

Empty road.

Burning Toyota.

And the sharp, kerosene-bite of Jet A fuel, not something the Toyota would have along. The *Menace,* truly dead, was leaking out her life's blood of highly combustible fuel where a hot exhaust port or turbine engine was bound to ignite it.

With an apology to the dead pilot, she set the timer on the self-destruct charges for thirty seconds and pulled the pin.

Amy climbed out, trying not to step on Bernie as she did so.

She wished she could think of some words to say. Or maybe take his rifle for backup, and any ammo she could grab. Or she could...*Get her ass moving!*

A part of her was counting.

Twenty. Her feet hit the ground.

Nineteen. She started running.

Eighteen and a half—her left leg collapsed beneath her.

"Not good!" she muttered. "Go! Go!" Her leg didn't seem inclined to answer her command.

By twelve she had her FN-SCAR rifle free and by ten the stock extended. *Faster!* It made for a lousy crutch, but by eight she was hobbling away again.

Along the road would be bad. No cover.

Climb the steep canyon wall that began close beside the helicopter?

Height was tactically good, but she didn't have it in her.

Instead she raced across the road.

Almost went down in a pothole the size of Kansas, but recovered.

At three, ignoring pain, she threw herself off the edge and rolled down the rocky embankment. She crashed into a large boulder close by the water—bad leg first, of course—trying not to scream aloud. The rock was all that kept her from falling into the rushing river.

At zero, the self-destruct charges pre-mounted on the MH-6M Little Bird *Menace* fired off. The charge under the console shredded the electronics and shattered the forward sensor array. The second charge, planted close beside the T63 turboshaft engine, destroyed the engine and the rotor shaft. The last two charges blew the two side-mounted miniguns and the unfired missiles to hell, which in turn ignited all of the missiles still in their housing.

"One kick-ass funeral pyre, Bernie. Sorry, best I could do." Amy spoke from where she'd managed to get behind a boulder and wait out the rolling wave of fire—a scorching heat she could feel through her heavy flightsuit and the transparent helmet visor. Even with her eyes pressed shut and overloaded with stars of pain from her leg, the flash was bright enough to hurt.

When the initial blast was done, she lay there a moment longer.

Five years she'd flown with the 101st Airborne and had never lost a craft. Two more years of intensive training after SOAR had accepted her into the Night Stalkers, still no. And on her first flight as a mission-qualified co-pilot, she was lying wounded along a river in an enemy country where her life expectancy was suddenly very, very short.

And her helo was rapidly turning into charred garbage.

They'd assigned Bernie and her to fly rear guard because it was the safest position for her initial sortie.

Right.

Hell of a first day.

Dusty would laugh himself sick when she told him about it.

CHAPTER 3

Chief Warrant Officer Dusty James was as furious as he thought only Amy could make him.

"That's my wife back there," he snarled at Lola Maloney, the commander of the 5th Battalion D Company. She was flying just five rotors ahead of him.

"It's up to CSAR. Get off the air," she snapped back.

"Combat Search and Rescue, my ass," he cursed at the radio, though without hitting transmit. Lola Maloney had flown CSAR before she went Night Stalkers, so she was biased in their favor.

It didn't help in the slightest that she was right. And that he shouldn't have risked the radio transmission even on an encrypted channel.

Already the spot where Amy had dropped off the tactical data feed on the inside of his visor was miles behind them, and the enemy in front of them couldn't be allowed to gain more ground. He kept his Black Hawk moving at the V-max speed and dove down into the heart of the pass.

They crossed over into Iran at three meters above the rocky soil. He had a fireteam of four U.S. Rangers and pair of

Delta operators aboard. They were all headed to cut off the head of an extremist cell that was racing to a refuge in a country where the U.S. didn't dare follow.

Iran had insisted that it could deal with its own problems, but the last few incursions by jihadists from behind the "Hijab Curtain" had gone undetected. Terrorists would strike at the Iraqis, then rush to the Iranian border. There they'd pull on women's clothes including the head covering of a *hijab* complete with a veil. They'd then cross the border—undetected by the male guards who were forbidden by Islamic Law from touching another man's woman.

If the terrorists made it over the last tortuous ten kilometers of road from the border, they would disappear into the quarter of a million people in the city of Piranshahr, Iran.

Tonight they wouldn't be getting away with that. Especially because America's Number Three Most Wanted was in the group.

But Amy—

She had to be alive. No question there, Dusty reassured himself. Too good a pilot, too much of a survivor.

He nosed down and crept a few rotors closer to LaRue's helo.

Get this strike done and then he was going back to find her, no matter what anyone said.

CHAPTER 4

*O*nce her hearing recovered from the blast of destroying her own helicopter, Amy paused to assess.

Left leg stung like a son of a bitch. Another reason to imagine Dusty laughing. He was the calm one who seldom swore. He'd hardly even cursed when she'd punched him on their first meeting in Portland, Oregon, and landed him in a bed of thorny rose bushes where an old willow tree had stood.

She was definitely the one with the temper.

First assessment. She heard nothing but the occasional unexploded round cooking off with a bang: two from the helo, one from the truck still blazing a few hundred meters down the road, then another spatter from the helo.

No other vehicle sounds. If anyone was hunting her, they were doing it quietly on foot. She'd thought the night-vision gear had been a write-off, but her final dive had merely knocked it aside. She repositioned the four lens system, three of which were still working.

Rocky valley. Rushing river a dozen meters wide. A lot of

rocks and little growth. There were still two heat blooms up over the lip of the embankment.

Second assessment. Her calf still hurt like...*Yeah, Dusty. About like that.* She inspected the hole in her flightsuit. No massive entry hole like the 23mm that had bored through Bernie's helmet.

Only a 9mm. Exit hole the same size behind her calf. No blood pouring out or squishing down into her boot, so it wasn't arterial. She'd been able to walk, which meant the bone was intact. At least before she'd slammed it into the boulder.

Meat shot. A lucky shot that had slid in through the non-existent door while she was maneuvering; too hyped on adrenaline to feel it. Until now! Holy crap it hurt!

She pulled a medical wrap out of her first aid chest pouch. Bright white. She did not need to place a banner on her leg that said, "Shoot me here. Again. Please." But she didn't have time to peel out of the flightsuit and do this properly.

Stuffing away the bandage, she dug out a strip of matte-black hundred-mile-an-hour duct tape and wrapped her calf snugly. A quick check revealed no other signs or twinges of injury.

Okay, time to start surviving.

One. Don't be found anywhere near a burning helicopter because they tended to draw a lot of attention.

Again she listened.

Nothing.

She crawled up to pop her head over the edge of the embankment and scanned through her night-vision goggles.

No one...No one...

There!

A single figure on the road. He was staggering and there were the brighter patches of hot blood on his shirt. He must have been blown clear of the truck by the blast. If one was, another could have been. The odds didn't look good.

So, Amy slid down the rubble bank toward the river that flowed briskly with the combination of melting snow and a recent spring rain.

She tightened all the cuffs on her flightsuit to keep out as much water as possible and slid down into the water. While she was at it, she flipped the Velcro covers off the infrared reflector tabs built into her uniform's shoulders so that they'd show. They'd reflect back an infrared dot into any night-vision gear, if someone who possessed some went looking for her.

Holy shit it was cold!

Saddle up, girl!

She took a deep breath and let the current carry her away.

CHAPTER 5

Focus, Dusty. Focus! You aren't any good to her dead.

SOAR made its living in darkness and so close to the ground that no other pilot would risk the same route, not even in broad daylight. It took immense concentration, a highly trained light touch on the controls, and lightning fast reflexes. He wasn't having any trouble with the latter two.

The first was being a real issue.

CSAR had arrived on the scene behind them. They reported one dead truck, one dead helo burned past recognition, and one dead enemy soldier, still clutching his rifle, bled out in the middle of the road halfway between the two.

The cockpit of the helo only had one body in it, they thought, but it was impossible to tell for sure. No way at all to tell if it was Bernie or Amy.

No other sign.

They collected what scrap they could, had tied the biggest remaining chunks of helo that might be identifiable as American onto a long line, and hauled ass back out to

Turkey. The U.S. forces weren't even supposed to be in this part of Iraq anymore, never mind Iran.

Iran.

Focus, Dusty. Focus!

"There!" he called out a half second ahead of his co-pilot. A trio of vehicles moving fast less than two kilometers from, and closing on, the city's edge.

"Get me alongside the lead vehicle," the Delta Force operator called over the intercom from the rear of Dusty's Black Hawk.

"Let me just shoot a rocket into each of their—" but Dusty was already moving into place.

"Won't achieve the objective," and Dusty knew the Delta operator was right.

The primary objective was to stop these guys at all costs. The secondary was to not let it look like it was done by the Americans. A trio of Hellfire missiles would disintegrate the vehicles in an immensely satisfying cloud of shrapnel. But they would also cut craters several meters deep into the road and probably spark an international incident.

Dusty positioned his Black Hawk alongside the lead vehicle, a hundred meters upslope into the darkness and hugging the terrain. This is why his bird was on this mission. Lola Maloney flew the DAP Hawk, the massively weaponized version of his transport bird. He carried personnel: Delta and Ranger shooters. For the moment, this operation was his.

"Steady," was all the Delta said as Dusty held position on the lead. He chose a line of flight that would not intersect the hillside nor lift him up into Iranian radar and smoothed out on the flight controls.

The vehicles were racing flat-out toward a sharp hairpin curve high on the hillside above the town. Dusty came in as close as he dared, estimating the volume of their roaring engines versus his pounding rotors.

Over the intercom he heard the sharp spit of a rifle. Once, twice, three times.

Each in turn, the vehicles swerved badly, right at the heart of the hairpin. Instead of making the corner, the vehicles launched—one after another—off the end of the curve and out into space. After a long fall, they landed in a single heap, or close enough. One caught on fire and the blaze jumped rapidly from vehicle to vehicle. One of the gas tanks exploded.

Through his night-vision, Dusty could see no figures on the move. No one had survived the crash in good enough shape to escape the fire.

"Oh, shooting the drivers in the head is so much more subtle." He couldn't help harassing the Delta operator. He'd wanted, he'd *needed*, the satisfaction of blowing the crap out of them himself.

"I shot the left front tire as each initiated their hairpin turn," the operator replied. "It is unlikely that will be noticed in the aftermath."

Okay, Dusty had to admit that was pretty slick.

They watched the blaze for another twenty seconds, but still no sign of any survivors.

Without waiting for instructions, Dusty spun the Black Hawk and pounded back toward the Iraqi border. And Amy.

CHAPTER 6

*A*my rode the icy current, cursed the rocks, especially the ones that kept insisting on hitting her bad leg. With each impact, it felt more and more like ice was invading her blood and soon her frozen bones would shatter.

A stream joined the river and the speed picked up. When it flattened, she swam. When it sped through quick rapids, she did what she could to protect her bad leg.

The CSAR craft shot by close overhead and she grabbed her radio: no lights, no action.

She struggled to the muddy bank and a patch of trees. Pulling out a penlight, she saw they were willow trees. It gave her a moment of vertigo-*how were they here but Dustin wasn't? Hadn't they courted under a willow? But was it this one? It's leaves were yellow with autumn. But their tree had been winter bare, hadn't it?* Amy recognized the signs of impending shock and forced herself to inspect the problem.

The problem was that a second 9mm round—one going for her left breast—Dusty's favorite—had smithereened the radio instead. It was hard to be angry about it. The armor in her vest should have protected her as well, but it would have left one hell of a bruise. And that was if she was lucky.

Lucky.

Two years ago she'd met Dusty in the Portland, Oregon, rose garden. The same week she'd started SOAR training. Best two things that had ever happened to her. Too much luck spent there, perhaps. Not enough left over for now when she really needed it.

Two years married but spent mostly apart, together only when they could both get leave. And finally, assigned together to the 5th Battalion D Company three days ago— the only outfit she knew of in the U.S. Armed Forces that ever allowed couples to serve together.

And now she was wounded and alone in a mud bank along an Iraqi river.

Great honeymoon dear. Just perfect.

CHAPTER 7

*D*ustin tried not to think about the tactical readout. There should only be two helos on it; himself and Lola Maloney.

But the readout showed that behind them the Iranians were already up in the air, climbing out of Piranshahr. Thankfully they were too late to see the Black Hawks. Perhaps they would be distracted by the three burning vehicles off the final hairpin turn above the city and not go looking for American phantoms.

He and Lola had their Hawks across the border before the first Iranian helos had even reached the city limits.

However, he could see that up ahead the Iraqis were also airborne and inbound from the west. No one, especially the President of the United States, wanted to be explaining a multiple helicopter incursion by U.S. forces so close to the Iranian border.

"One sweep of the area," Lola said over the radio. "Then we're gone."

She was right, one sweep was all they had time for.

CHAPTER 8

*L*ying in the mud, Amy calculated her chances and they didn't look good. She'd floated too close to a town and didn't know if she'd survive getting back in the water to float further downstream.

The batteries in her night-vision gear were dying.

It was cold and the seals on her flightsuit were never meant to replace scuba gear. Shivers were shaking her badly, making it hard to think and to use her hands.

She managed to dig out the emergency satellite radio and send off a single squirt. Not knowing who was in the area, she didn't dare do more.

The batteries in the NVGs died and she might as well be blind. She had more batteries somewhere. Or it seemed she should. In her vest? Thigh pouch? It was getting hard to concentrate. She pulled off her helmet and set it in the mud beside her.

Darkness.

CHAPTER 9

*D*ustin found the last flickers of the burning truck, the dead man in the middle of the road, and the blackened patch surrounded by a wide debris field of tiny bits of Little Bird helicopter.

He spun down to land nearby and took the risk of calling Amy's name over the PA mounted on the undercarriage of his machine.

The two Delta shooters hopped out and scouted the ground, first around the burnout spot then farther afield. They snapped to like a pair of Irish Setters and disappeared out of sight over the river embankment.

Twenty seconds later they rushed back onto the helicopter.

Dustin pulled up into the air—parking on an Iraqi highway where two explosions had just occurred with the Iraqi Army on the way was nuts even by SOAR standards.

"The river," the Delta operator spoke as soon as he was back on the intercom. "Blood close by the bank—"

Dustin felt ill and clamped his teeth together.

"—but probably not arterial. Follow the water."

Dustin dropped down into the canyon and eased forward, trusting Lola to watch his back. He wanted to creep slowly so that he could search more carefully, but he was too aware of the impending arrival of the Iraqi forces. His head commanded his heart, so he pushed ahead as fast as he dared. His hand ached on the cyclic as if it knew it would never again hold—

He slammed the thought aside and watched the river.

Every branch caught in the current startled him, as did every ripple and bend. A deer who had wandered down to the river for a drink shone like a blazing hot neon sign in his night-vision gear and just about shocked Dustin to death.

But it wasn't her.

He edged as close as he dared to a town, but there was nothing except some old willow trees dropping down over the bank.

They were going to have to send in a ground SAR team. The chances of them finding...

Amy had to be alive or he'd be lost.

CHAPTER 10

*A*my heard a pair of helicopters approaching.

The heavy beat of their rotors was almost as deep as the river's rushing waters.

She tried to dig out of the brush bower she'd gathered over herself beneath the trees. Somewhere along the way she'd lost even that much capacity.

It turned out not to matter. Before they reached her, they turned away and were gone.

Amy curled up half on the brush, half under. Too exhausted to burrow back beneath the protective layer. She used what memories she could of Dustin to keep her warm.

But all she could recall was the gray Oregon rain on the frigid December day when they first met.

CHAPTER 11

Dustin was just ten kilometers north of the river on the way back to Turkey when the call came in, transmitted from Fort Campbell, Kentucky, via satellite.

"Nine Vee," tonight's code for the mission, "we just received a satellite radio burst from your vicinity. We have an approximate location a couple hundred meters east of Drybnd, but can't make sense of it."

Dustin did his best to keep his hope under control.

"It was a single word: Willow."

Dustin slammed over the cyclic. Laying every bit of five thousand horsepower the twin T700 turboshaft engines could throw into ten tons of helo, he ran his speed right up against the Never Exceed limit.

He and Amy had met because of one willow tree being cut down and been married in front of the replacement they had planted together.

CHAPTER 12

$\mathcal{A}$my came to as they rushed her from beneath her tree toward a waiting helicopter.

"Dusty?"

"Here, babe," said the man crushing her hand in his.

"You found my willow tree, just like that first day when we met."

"Always will," he promised her as she slid back toward sleep. "Every day."

It was good. Dusty always kept his promises.

GHOST OF WILLOW'S PAST

(EXCERPT)

aster Sergeant Dustin James nudged a clod of dirt back into place with the toe of his boot. The rich black soil of the Portland Oregon Rose Garden simply dissolved and left a blackish patch of mud on the worn leather. Today was the Winter Solstice. It was raining and about three degrees above freezing. Pretty typical. He stared down at the *Rosa canina*.

This rose had been propagated from a cutting of the oldest documented rose bush on the planet. The rose now huddled, dormant and pruned back for the winter. In bloom, it was the least assuming rose in the garden, a single layer of five pink petals around a yellow center. Four days before Christmas, it was a cluster of frosty twigs decorated by bright red rose hips.

Most people passed it by, but not his father, the head gardener of the nearby Japanese Garden. He had visited the rose every day after work on his walk home. Dusty and his mother had often walked up to meet him at the old Briar Rose.

"I met your mother by this rose. We married right here."

Being a man of few words, his father never embellished the story. It wasn't the most scenic spot in the garden, but with ten thousand rose bushes in a couple hundred neatly tended beds, not bad either. The fact that they'd married here on the Winter Solstice when nothing bloomed had been a little odd perhaps, but then his parents had been rather eccentric.

Dusty had come home for this Christmas, even though his parents had been gone for three years. Their small condo now lay empty most of the year due to a crashed tourist helicopter. An old Bell 206 called in an engine failure and then auto-rotated right into an Icelandic volcano, no survivors.

That Dusty was a crew chief and mechanic on a Sikorsky Black Hawk for the U.S. Army's 160th SOAR had made the loss beyond ironic. His job was to fly, fight, and keep the Special Operations Aviation Regiment choppers running perfectly despite war conditions. His parents had died, probably from a broken fan belt.

So, any time that he was home, but especially on the Winter Solstice, he made a point of coming to visit their rose as his parents had done so often for their three decades together.

"I'm glad you went together, at least you got that much," he told the sleeping rose. With no ashes to scatter, he'd gathered some ash from the volcano and scattered it onto the rose's soil. His parents belonged together here. His father, a quiet man who loved visiting the garden's roses, such a contrast to his artistic Japanese garden, and his wild mother, a true child of the sixties, who had never understood Dusty's choice to serve. They appeared such an oddly-matched couple, the slight Eurasian and the tall, busty blonde.

"She brings me to life like the spring warmth."

"He keeps me steady with his deep roots."

When would Dusty find that? His own dreams had just

been pruned back hard. He'd found out, on no notice, that he had a week's leave. He'd rushed back to Portland only to discover that Nancy had meant to Dear Dusty him, but forgotten, as usual, to follow through. Another woman who hadn't understood his need to serve his country, his need to protect that which was so precious. She was living with some software geek named Ralph.

Dusty's few friends still in the area were busy with pre-holiday family stuff. Some invited him over for a meal, but being a third wheel in some other couple's holiday wasn't his first choice, nor his second or third.

On call, Dusty really didn't have time to go anywhere els—

The cry of pain echoing across the garden snapped him out of his damp reverie. His Special Forces training had him sprinting down the garden path before he even fully registered what was happening.

One hand slapped for his sidearm, and came away empty. The other slapped for the med kit on his SARVSO survival vest, but he wore only a rain slick over his heavy sweater.

The cry sounded again, a woman in agonizing pain. Halfway across the garden from his parents' rose, he spotted the source. Not that it was hard. On a rainy, winter Friday morning there was only one other person in the garden.

She knelt in the mud at the edge of a garden bed.

Dusty rushed up beside her. "Where are you hurt?" Seeing no obvious wounds he started unzipping her parka.

Her punch came out of nowhere.

She hit him square in the solar plexus so fast he had no time to block it. He tumbled backward among the pruned roses, the thorns carving painful scratches across his cheek and bare hands.

"What the hell are you doing?" the woman shouted down at him. Her hands were poised to strike another blow. He recognized a Taekwondo black belt when he met one and held his hands palm out.

Dusty rolled slowly from the rose bushes onto the wet grass and inspected his hands. "Ow! Shit, that hurts," he flexed a hand and felt every little scratch.

"Answer the damned question!"

He eyed her more carefully. It wasn't your average woman who issued commands to men half-again their size. He blinked the rain from his eyes. She had well-defined cheek bones, arched eyebrows that indicated brunette hair would be hiding under her hood, and eyes the brown of autumn leaves. He shook his head to clear it.

"You sounded like you'd been shot."

"Soldier?" She watched him closely.

"Yes."

She settled back on her heels in perfect balance, clearly poised so that she could attack easily if she decided it was needed.

"Okay. Maybe."

She puffed out a breath.

"I'm fine."

"You look fine, but you didn't sound it." She did look fine. Not the white of porcelain, but refinement shone in her features. He considered mentioning how much he'd love to draw those features with the artist pencils his mother had given to him as a young child. He didn't know if he'd ever seen so much personality in a woman's features before. It was a face made to laugh and smile, but was now drawn grim and closed.

"I..." In the single word he heard all of the wounded distress return to her voice. She glanced back at the bed of roses she knelt in.

"They cut down the tree," she whispered as softly as the rain.

Dusty looked around, trying to picture this part of the garden in his memory. A tree had been here, a big one.

"It was their willow tree."

That was it.

She pressed the heel of her palm against the center of chest.

"It makes my heart hurt."

ABOUT THE AUTHOR

M.L. Buchman started the first of, what is now over 50 novels and as many short stories, while flying from South Korea to ride his bicycle across the Australian Outback. Part of a solo around the world trip that ultimately launched his writing career.

All three of his military romantic suspense series—The Night Stalkers, Firehawks, and Delta Force—have had a title named "Top 10 Romance of the Year" by the American Library Association's *Booklist*. NPR and Barnes & Noble have named other titles "Top 5 Romance of the Year." In 2016 he was a finalist for Romance Writers of America prestigious RITA award. He also writes: contemporary romance, thrillers, and fantasy.

Past lives include: years as a project manager, rebuilding and single-handing a fifty-foot sailboat, both flying and jumping out of airplanes, and he has designed and built two houses. He is now making his living as a full-time writer on the Oregon Coast with his beloved wife and is constantly amazed at what you can do with a degree in Geophysics. You may keep up with his writing and receive a free starter e-library by subscribing to his newsletter at: www.mlbuchman.com

Other works by M. L. Buchman:

<u>The Night Stalkers</u>
MAIN FLIGHT
The Night Is Mine
I Own the Dawn
Wait Until Dark
Take Over at Midnight
Light Up the Night
Bring On the Dusk
By Break of Day
WHITE HOUSE HOLIDAY
Daniel's Christmas
Frank's Independence Day
Peter's Christmas
Zachary's Christmas
Roy's Independence Day
Damien's Christmas
AND THE NAVY
Christmas at Steel Beach
Christmas at Peleliu Cove
5E
Target of the Heart
Target Lock on Love
Target of Mine

<u>Firehawks</u>
MAIN FLIGHT
Pure Heat
Full Blaze
Hot Point
Flash of Fire
Wild Fire
SMOKEJUMPERS
Wildfire at Dawn
Wildfire at Larch Creek
Wildfire on the Skagit

<u>Delta Force</u>
Target Engaged
Heart Strike
Wild Justice

<u>Where Dreams</u>
Where Dreams are Born
Where Dreams Reside
Where Dreams Are of Christmas
Where Dreams Unfold
Where Dreams Are Written

<u>Eagle Cove</u>
Return to Eagle Cove
Recipe for Eagle Cove
Longing for Eagle Cove
Keepsake for Eagle Cove

<u>Henderson's Ranch</u>
Nathan's Big Sky

<u>Love Abroad</u>
Heart of the Cotswolds: England

<u>Dead Chef Thrillers</u>
Swap Out!
One Chef!
Two Chef!

<u>Deities Anonymous</u>
Cookbook from Hell: Reheated
Saviors 101

<u>SF/F Titles</u>
The Nara Reaction
Monk's Maze
the Me and Elsie Chronicles

<u>Strategies for Success (NF)</u>
Managing Your Inner Artist/Writer
Estate Planning for Authors

www.ingramcontent.com/pod-product-compliance
Lightning Source LLC
Chambersburg PA
CBHW030027200726
48283CB00012B/1345